love! —L.N.

—F.B.

If You Give a Cat a Cupcake

If You Give a

Cat a Cupcake

WRITTEN BY Laura Numeroff

ILLUSTRATED BY Felicia Bond

SCHOLASTIC INC.
New York Toronto London Auckland
Sydney Mexico City New Delhi Hong Kong

ISBN 978-0-545-42235-2

Text copyright © 2008 by Laura Numeroff. Illustrations copyright © 2008 by Felicia Bond. All rights reserved. Published by Scholastic Inc., 557 Broadway, New York, NY 10012, by arrangement with HarperCollins Children's Books, a division of HarperCollins Publishers. SCHOLASTIC and associated logos are trademarks and/or registered trademarks of Scholastic Inc.

12 11 10 9 8 7 6 5   11 12 13 14 15 16/0

Printed in the U.S.A.   40

First Scholastic printing, September 2011

  is a registered trademark of HarperCollins Publishers

If you give a cat a cupcake,

he'll ask for some sprinkles to go with it.

When you give him the sprinkles,
he might spill some on the floor.

Cleaning up will make him hot,
so you'll give him a bathing suit

and take him to the beach.

He'll want to go in the water

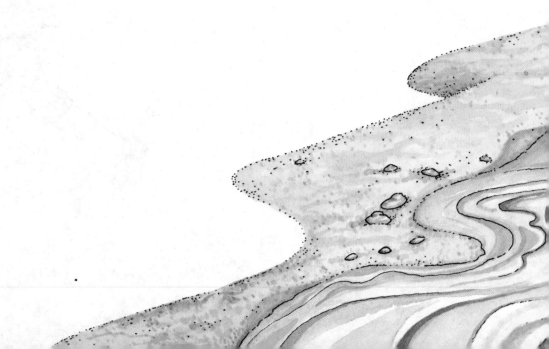

and build a sand castle, too.

Then he'll look for seashells.

He'll find a few other things as well.

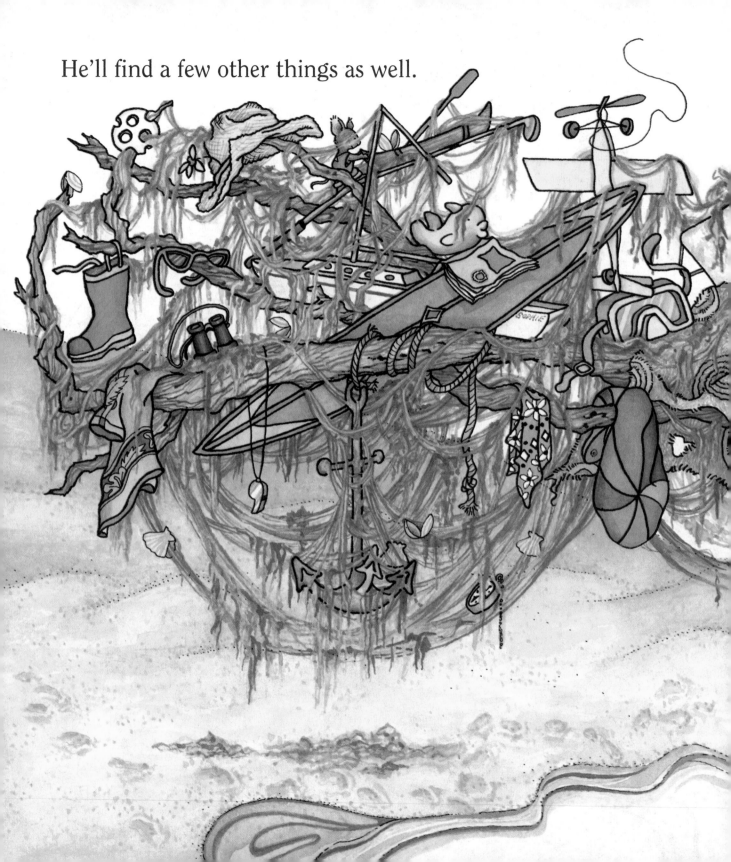

He'll put them in his pail and try to pick it up,
but it'll be too heavy.

He'll decide he needs to work out at the gym.

First he'll warm up on the treadmill.

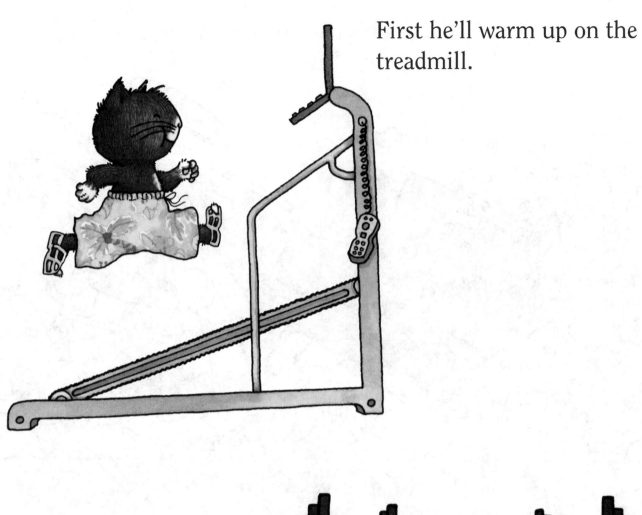

Then he'll lift a weight or two.

He might even try a karate class.

After the gym, he'll want to go to the park.
When you get there, he'll see the rocks.
He'll climb as high as he can go.

At the top, he'll see the lake.
He'll want you to take him rowing.

He'll be the captain,
and you'll have to row.

Then he'll notice the merry-go-round
and want to go for a ride.

He'll want you to go for a ride, too.

You'll choose the horse with the purple mane,
and he'll get on the whale.

The whale will remind him
of the science museum.
He'll ask you to take him there.

First he'll find the

dinosaurs.

Then he'll visit the

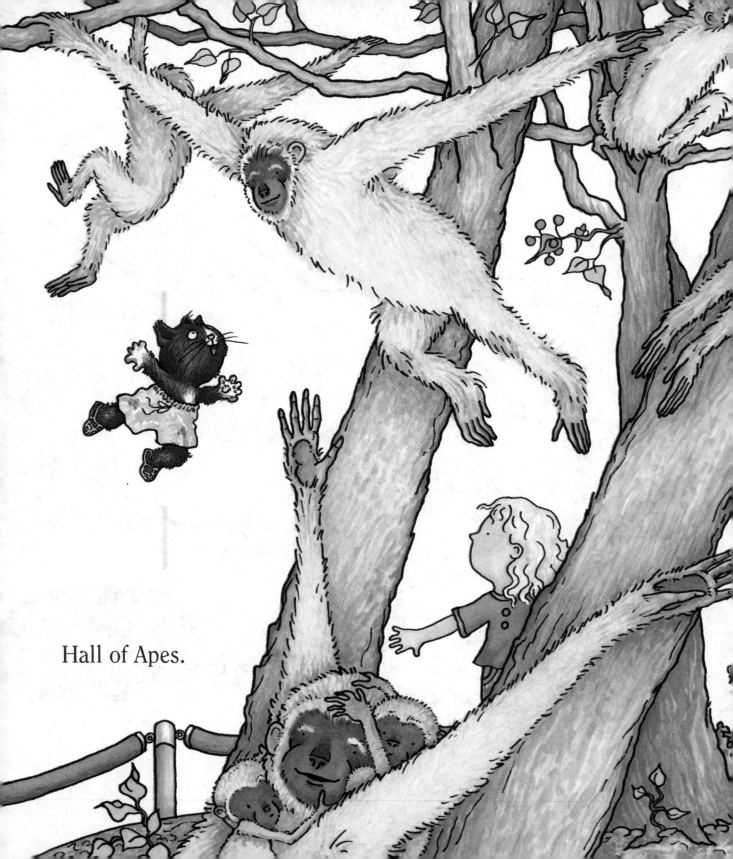

Hall of Apes.

When the museum closes,
you'll be the last to leave.

On the way home, you'll pass by the beach.
You'll help him gather all of his things.

Then he'll want to race you.

When you get home, he'll empty
the sand from his shoes.
He might spill some on the floor.

Seeing the sand on the floor
will remind him of the sprinkles.

He'll probably ask you for some.

And chances are,

if you give him some sprinkles,

he'll want a cupcake to go with them.